Bright ≡Summaries.com

The Princess of Cleves

by Madame de Lafayette

BOOK ANALYSIS

Written by Fabienne Gheysens
Translated by Oliver Brown

The Princess of Cleves

by Madame de Lafayette

MADAME DE LA FAYETTE

- **Born in 1634 in Paris**
- **Died in 1693 in the same town**
- **Some of his works:**
  - *The Princess of Montpensier* (1662), novel
  - *Zayde* (1669-1671), novel
  - *The Princess of Cleves* (1678), novel

Marie-Magdeleine Pioche de la Vergne, known as Countess de la Fayette, was born on 18 March 1634 and died of heart disease on 25 May 1693 in Paris. She was the daughter of a gentleman of minor nobility. Her father died in 1649, and her mother remarried to a man named Renaud de Sévigné, uncle of the Marquise de Sévigné (French woman of letters, 1626-1696). Marie Magdeleine became friends with the latter, who invited her to frequent the court society and literary salons of the time. There, she met Jean-François Motier, Count de la Fayette, whom she married. Married without love, the couple ran out of steam, and the Count de la Fayette decided to retire to the countryside, leaving his wife in Paris.

In the literary salons, the countess met La Rochefoucauld (French writer, 1613-1680) with whom she formed a close and long-lasting friendship. Through this relationship, she became immersed in the world of the literati. From then on, Racine (1639-1699), Corneille (1606-1684) and many others became the authors Marie-Magdeleine read and heard.

During these years spent in this society of scholars, she first wrote two stories: *La Princesse de Montpensier* (1662) and *Zaïde* (1670), which perfectly illustrate the literary themes of her time. However, Mme de la Fayette sought to innovate, and with the help of La Rochefoucauld, turned to a style of writing marked by history and accuracy. She wrote *Histoire d'Henriette d'Angleterre*, the memoirs of the British princess Henriette (1644-1660). In 1678, she published *The Princess of Cleves*: the work, of a genre difficult to define because it is halfway between the historical novel and the analytical novel, was a huge success. It is part of a new literary school and is, as such, considered to be the first book that corresponds to the modern conception of the novel.

THE PRINCESS OF CLEVES

A NOVEL ABOUT PASSION

- **Genre:** novel

- **Reference edition:** *La Princesse de Clèves*, Paris, Librairie Générale Française, 1999, 256 p.

- **1re edition:** 1678

- **Themes:** fidelity, dilemma, adultery, reputation, passion

The novel, written in collaboration with Segrais (French poet, 1624-1701) and La Rochefoucauld, was published anonymously in 1678, as Mme de La Fayette expressly refused to be attributed with it, as it was incompatible with her sex and rank. On its publication, the work was the subject of a clever press campaign in *Le Mercure galant*, which contributed to its success; a success that would not be denied throughout the centuries, many considering it to be the first modern psychological novel.

The Princess of Cleves recounts the conflict that torments the eponymous heroine, struggling between the loyalty she owes to her husband and the destructive love passion she represses towards the Duke of Nemours.

SUMMARY

PART 1

In 1558, a beautiful 16-year-old girl appeared at the court of Henry II (King of France, 1519-1559): Mlle de Chartres. Fatherless, she was accompanied by her mother, who had educated her.

Marriage plans between various members of the court fail due to intrigues. The Prince of Cleves proposes to Mlle de Chartres. The young woman consents to this marriage of convenience, thus becoming the Princess of Cleves. She and her mother assume that tenderness and time will make married love blossom.

At a ball given by the king, the princess meets the Duke of Nemours. An all-consuming passion is born between them, but it remains hidden.

As Mme de Chartres lies dying, her daughter tells her of her feelings for Nemours. The mother implores her daughter to give up this passion, which she fears will cause her harm. Mme de Clèves then decides to retire to the countryside, to Coulommiers.

PART TWO

There, Mme de Clèves learns of the death of Mme de Tournon, a woman she admired. The Prince of Cleves tells her an anecdote: one of his friends, M. de Sancerre, had been in love with Mme de Tournon for two years, and she had secretly promised to marry him. However, on the day of her death, M. de Sancerre discovered some passionate letters which were not addressed to him; Mme de Tournon had in fact made the same speech to M. d'Estouville. M. de Sancerre was extremely upset. The Prince of Cleves drew a general conclusion from this story: it is better for a married woman to confess some inclination elsewhere than to hide it from her husband; the latter would not be upset, as he would not have the unpleasant surprise of a disclosed affair. The princess was deeply disturbed by these last words.

The Prince of Cleves convinces his wife to follow him to Paris. She realises that she still has feelings for the Duke of Nemours. For his part, Nemours has given up his hopes of an English crown for the love he had for her. The Princess of Cleves tries to control her emotions and wants to flee again.

One day, she realises that Nemours is stealing a portrait of her. However, she remains silent, for fear of revealing the Duke's passion publicly and in order not to incite him to declare his love. But Nemours realises that the princess has observed the scene, but has not denounced him. He returns home happy, knowing he is loved.

During a tournament, the duke risks injury. The worried look in Mme de Clèves' eyes is unequivocal. The Chevalier de Guise, who is also in love with the princess, sees this and understands that he has no chance of winning her;

he goes on an adventure, far from France, and will die abroad.

One day, the princess intercepts a letter from a woman who is circulating in the court and who suggests that Nemours is having an affair. Mme de Clèves feels jealousy rising within her.

PART THREE

In reality, the letter was intended for the vidame de Chartres, the uncle of the princess and confidant of the queen. He risked a great deal if he was identified; his lover would be compromised and the queen would reproach him for this adventure. The vidame then charged the Duc de Nemours with a mission; to pass himself off as the recipient of the letter.

Nemours visits Mme de Clèves and proves his good faith. In this way, he dispels the princess' jealousy and recovers the letter. Nemours passes it on to the vidame, who returns it to his lover. However, the Dauphine also claimed the note that had caused the trouble. It is therefore necessary to copy it from memory. In the presence of M. de Clèves, the princess and the duke rewrite the letter. They enjoy this moment of intimacy. However, the imitation is imperfect, and the queen senses the deception. The vidame thus loses her esteem.

Once again worried by the passion she feels for the Duke, the Princess goes back to Coulommiers. Her husband reproaches her for her taste for solitude. She then confesses her love for another man. She says she has to get away from the court to remain worthy of her husband. At first, he recognises her sincere loyalty, but then he cannot help but press her with jealous questions. However, she does not reveal the name of her lover. Nemours, in hiding, witnessed the scene.

Shortly afterwards, the king asks the Prince of Cleves to return to Paris. Alone at home, the princess is frightened by his confession, but she convinces herself that she has remained faithful to her husband.

Nemours is divided; he understands that this confession puts an end to any hope of securing the princess's favour, but he is delighted to love and be loved in return. He cannot restrain his desire to tell the story to his friend the vidame. Despite the duke's evasive and imprecise speech, the vidame understands that it is indeed his friend who is in question. Through this imprudence, the story becomes public. The Prince and the Princess of Cleves accuse each other of having disclosed their conversation, unaware that Nemours had overheard them.

The king dies during a tournament.

PART FOUR

The court goes to Reims for the coronation of the new king. Meanwhile, the princess remains in Coulommiers. Nemours observes her at night, as she contemplates a painting of him. This encourages him to join her. Thinking she recognises him in the garden, she flees to another room in the castle. Nemours waits in vain and decides to return the following night. However, Nemours was followed by a spy in the pay of the Prince of Cleves. On hearing the news, the Prince is convinced that his wife has deceived him. He dies of grief while blaming his wife.

Terrified, the princess refuses to see the duke again. The vidame finally manages to arrange a secret meeting between the two lovers. Nemours confesses that he was the one who made the revelation. The Princess of Cleves rejects the Duke and leaves without him being able to keep her. She goes into exile in the Pyrenees and takes holy orders. Seriously ill, she died there a few years later.

CHARACTER STUDY

MME OF CHARTRES

The heroine's mother, Mme de Chartres, determines the whole plot. Coming from the provinces, she goes to the court to look for a husband for her daughter. She embodies the moral and aristocratic values of previous decades: respect for marital duty, the importance of reputation, etc.

She is accompanied by her daughter, Mlle de Chartres, whom she has raised in a strict and virtuous environment. She wants her to stand out from the crowd of other women and determine her course, making her the agent of her personal plan.

She relentlessly pursues this goal, this programme, this burden, even on her deathbed. After hearing her daughter's confession of her feelings for Nemours, Mme de Chartres does not hesitate to resort to emotional blackmail: filial love serves as a last defence against passion. For example, during the final farewell, she declares:

> *"Think of what you owe to your husband; think of what you owe to yourself, and think that you are going to lose this reputation that you have acquired and that I have wished so much for you. Have strength and courage, my daughter, withdraw from the court [...]. If reasons other than those of virtue and your duty could oblige you to do what I wish, I would tell you that, if anything were capable of disturbing the happiness I hope for on leaving this world, it would be to see you fall like other women; but, if this misfortune should befall you, I welcome death with joy, so as not*

Beyond death, the mother's honour rests on her daughter's conduct. The farewell ratifies a whole process of guilt. In a way, the mother and the author overlap: the mother seals her daughter's fate, just as the author fixes the fate of her heroine.

THE PRINCE OF CLEVES

The heroine's husband, the Prince of Cleves, deplores having provoked his wife's confession. Consumed with jealousy, he accuses her of adultery.

His death echoes that of Mme de Chartres. Here too, death follows confession, and the dying man declares that he finds death pleasant because of what he knows. Solemnly he proclaims:

The permission is only apparent. In fact, marrying the rival would bring the Princess of Cleves into irreversible disrepute. With these words, the prince challenges his wife to respect his memory. We can guess that she would never allow herself to be unworthy of her husband.

THE DUKE OF NEMOURS

The first pages of the novel include the Duke of Nemours among the most admirable men of the court. He is indeed presented as the most handsome, the most distinguished, etc. Naturally, the logic of the novel would like to associate him with the most beautiful and distinguished of women, namely our young heroine. But this assumption is contradicted: they meet, but too late, as the princess already has a husband.

Nemours is certainly young and handsome, but then we discover his true personality, disguised by convention: the duke is revealed as a seducer, opportunist and cynic.

THE VIDAME OF CHARTRES

The heroine's uncle, the vidame de Chartres, is compared to Nemours from the very first pages. Both personify the court through their gallantry. He is a sort of double of Nemours, whose past he recalls and whose future he announces.

An uncle and confidant of the Princess of Cleves, he could be considered a kind of substitute for the father figure.

MLLE DE CHARTRES/THE PRINCESS OF CLEVES

The heroine of the novel, the Princess of Cleves, is not, however, the master of her life. She is influenced by the other protagonists: her mother's authority, her husband's sensitivity, Nemours' seduction and the etiquette of the court.

The princess internalises her mother's precepts. She places two virtues above all others: sincerity, which guarantees her mission, and the control she exercises over her emotions. Taking advantage of these principles, she claims to sublimate the failings that threaten her. At the same time, she unconsciously sets herself up as an example to be admired and emulated. This results in a certain form of personal pride, even pride.

However, in some situations, sincerity and self-control are in deep conflict. The princess prefers to confess her shortcomings out of self-respect. Whenever she feels her will weakening, she confesses her wrongs. Will revealing her mistakes dissuade her from committing others? No doubt she hopes so. She thinks she is taming her own moods. In these stagings, feminine heroism and narcissism are mixed. But the princess assumes her strength. Each time, indecision persists. Each time, the fault gets worse.

Only the proximity of death keeps her from the passion that agitates her. By taking refuge in religion, she manages to preserve the ideal she has made her own. By renouncing the world, she finally honours her promises. But at what price?

KEYS TO READING

A WARNING AGAINST PASSION

Mme de La Fayette considers love passions to be fatal; she hates the troubles, jealousies, dissatisfactions and sorrows they engender. In comparison, moments of happiness would be all too fleeting. In this sense, the term "passion" comes close to its etymological meaning; suffering and pain.

The author opposes a different vision of love, influenced by the precious current, to heart-rending passion. She advocates a form of solid and benevolent sympathy, a sentimental and intellectual, friendly, and even platonic attachment. This union, cordial and unshakeable, soothes the heart and is a source of harmony. It is similar to Stoic ataraxia (the search for the absence of troubles). It is a question of blurring the ardour of passionate troubles to achieve self-control and emotional balance. Mme de La Fayette herself experienced this way of living love, first with Gilles Ménage (French writer, 1613-1692), then with La Rochefoucauld.

 PRECIOUSNESS

ᵉIt is a French literary phenomenon that originated in the 18th CENTURY in the salons of society where the art of conversation was practiced. Preciosity is characterised by a search for refinement, both in psychological analysis (especially of love) and in the way of expressing oneself (the precious reject vulgarity and try to distinguish themselves through pure language, but their language is so affected that it becomes incomprehensible).

In this story, the heroine cultivates an ideal vision of love. She seeks a sincere and lasting love, devoid of interest or ambition, capable of standing the test of time. She rejects ephemeral and impure liaisons.

But, curiously, the princess seems to be a stranger to the love of her husband, whose sensibility is close to her own. Little by little, she falls in love with the Duke of Nemours. This alienating passion hampers her intelligence: she does not directly perceive the significance of her actions, confesses her infidelity while insisting on keeping the name of the man she loves secret, etc. Finally, the heroine realizes the Duke of Nemours' indiscretion and bitterly realizes her failure:

> *"I was wrong to believe that there was a man capable of hiding what flatters his glory. Yet it is because of this man, whom I thought so different from the rest of men, that I find myself like other women, being so far from being like them. I have lost the heart and the esteem of a husband who was to have been my happiness. I shall soon be looked upon by everyone as a person who has a mad and violent passion. (p. 184)*

However, the various stories of passion that punctuate the novel – although by no means necessary for the action – were meant to warn the heroine of the risks of the latter: exaggerated idolatry, dissimulation, madness, etc. Vain warnings.

The princess understands that the reason why love wears out in marriage is that each person believes that the other is his or her own. She also understands that passion only lasts as long as the beloved (Nemours) escapes her. In short, she feels mediocre for having desired what she could not have. However, in spite of everything, only illness will weaken her passionate feelings, until the ultimate renunciation:

> "This long and imminent sight of death made Mme de Clèves see the things of this life with that eye which is so different when in health [...]. She overcame the remnants of that passion which had been weakened by the feelings that her illness had given her; thoughts of death had brought the memory of Monsieur de Clèves closer to her [...]. Finally, whole years having passed, time and absence slowed down her pain and extinguished her passion. Mme de Clèves lived in a way that left no appearance that she could ever return; she spent part of the year in this religious house and the other part at home, but in a retirement and in occupations holier than those of the most austere convents; and her life, which was rather short, left examples of inimitable virtues. (p. 236-239)

REFLEXIVE SLOW MOTION

Throughout the story, the princess oscillates between two postures:

- the poorly controlled action. Her gestures, her words, her blushes or her silences testify to her disorganised passion. She gives, in spite of herself, signs of her feelings;

- reflection. She takes time to reflect on her own behaviour. Assessments, nourished by repentance or remorse, lead to resolutions for the future. In short, a troubling event is always followed by a retrospective analysis.

Moreover, these two attitudes correspond to two spaces:

- public life, represented by the court (in Paris, in Blois) with its sumptuous ceremonies, its intrigues and its deceptive seductions;

- retreat, evoked by the countryside, private rooms, etc. Escaping from the world is necessary to meditate in peace. Whenever the need arises, the princess closes herself off in solitude.

In this third-person narrative, self-examination can take three forms:

- the psychological description, which sets out what is on the heroine's mind;

- the reported monologue, in which the speech of the princess to herself is presented in indirect style;

- the monologue in direct style.

These reflexive slow-motion sequences illustrate the princess's effort to see through her confusion. In order to escape the chaos of her passionate movements, she tries to unfold a discourse that reorganises her mind, that structures it. This is not a disordered mixture of confused impressions, nor a logorrhea of elusive ideas, but a linear, clear and coherent thought, enlightened by reason.

> *"[...] Mme de Clèves went home and locked herself in her study.*
>
> *It is impossible to express the pain she felt at knowing, from what her mother had just told her, the interest she took in M. de Nemours: she had not yet dared to admit it to herself. She then saw that the feelings she had for him were those which M. de Clèves had so much asked of her; she found how shameful it was to have them for another than for a husband who deserved them. She felt hurt and embarrassed by the fear that M. de Nemours would want to use her as a pretext for Mme the Dauphine and this thought determined her to tell Mme de Chartres what she had not yet told him. (p. 88-89)*

A "Cornelian" choice

The confession to the Duke of Nemours is precisely one of these reflexive slowdowns. The dilemma between duty and passion reveals the intimate character of the confession. This monologue is marked by the length of Mme de Clèves' reply compared to Nemours'. In addition, it is characterised by long sentences accompanied by a large number of relative clauses:

> *"I have told you too much to hide from you **that** you made it known to me and **that** I suffered such cruel pain **the** evening the Queen gave me this letter from Madame de Thémines, **which was** said to be addressed to you, **that** an idea of it has remained with me **which** makes me believe **that** it is the greatest of all evils. (end of the fourth part)*

The use of these long sentences highlights the slow thinking of the Princess of Cleves. Let us not forget that she is in the necessity of choosing between her duty and her passion. This shows that the character, as she speaks, is thinking about her final decision. This repetitive style allows us to perceive the character's hesitation.

In the end, there are many reflective phases in the novel, evidence of an intense personal journey. ^eThis also makes *The Princess of Cleves* a novel of apprenticeship, a genre that originated in Germany in the 18TH CENTURY, which traces the development of a hero.

GAMES OF LOOKS

In the novel, communication between individuals is indirect or very late. This explains the various forms of the verb 'to see' that are found throughout the novel.

Scenes of espionage and voyeurism

Symmetrical scenes are played out in places outside the court.

The protagonists are observed without their knowledge:

- Nemours spies on the princess from the window of a silk merchant;

- the princess finds Nemours asleep in a Parisian garden.

The spies themselves are contemplated:

- one of the lovers looks at the portrait of the other without knowing that the one he admires is observing him;

- the princess catches Nemours stealing a portrait of her;

- Nemours spies the princess in Coulommiers and finds her distressed at the sight of a painting she has procured. The painting depicts the siege of Metz, in which Nemours appears.

The court's view

At the court ball for the princely engagement, the king orders Mme de Clèves to dance with Nemours. This order has a symbolic significance: by seeing these two people as an acceptable couple, the king endorses an illegitimate union (pp. 71-72).

Moreover, through the etiquette it imposes, the court forces the characters to play a role, to shape a face that will be exposed to the eyes.

Be seen as an example

Finally, the princess assumes and overcomes the feeling of guilt and mediocrity that overwhelms her. She regains her self-respect and, if she meets Nemours one last time, it is because she asks him to report their conversation to the vidame de Chartres. In this way, she intends to arouse her uncle's admiration and set herself up as a model for him to emulate. From now on, by offering herself as an exemplary and irreproachable icon, she has a little more control over the gaze of others and frees herself from the role that the court was pushing her to play.

A confession out of sight of the court

The confession of the princess to the Duke of Nemours does not take place under the gaze of the court. Indeed, it is neither at court, characterised by its social codes, nor at the private and intimate home of Mme de Clèves that they meet, but in a neutral place that cannot influence their behaviour. The confession of feelings and the announcement of departure can thus be revealed freely, without tension from the outside and in a sincere manner. Since the characters are in a place outside the court, the princess banishes all the codes of society in order to free herself from her burden: "[...] I'm going to skip over all the restraint and delicacy I should have in a first conversation." (p. 230)

She thus takes the liberty of getting rid of everything that might prevent her, within society, from showing her feelings. From now on, she no longer takes into account the decorum that condemns the confession of a passion.

IS THE RETIREMENT OF THE PRINCESS OF CLEVES A FATALITY?

An ephemeral passion

This confession also serves as a social argument to convince herself that the only way to escape the situation she finds herself in is to withdraw from the court. Also, the Princess of Cleves fears that the Duke of Nemours' unexpected feelings will dissipate with time and the sight of other women: 'But do men retain passion in these eternal engagements? Shall I hope for a miracle in my favour [...]?

With this rhetorical question, the Princess of Cleves gives Nemours no alternative. He cannot deny these statements. Moreover, the term 'miracle' highlights the marginality of permanent love and the inescapable fate of married women.

This fear of ephemeral passion is the first argument that counterbalances the absence of obstacles to the love of the princess and Nemours. Mme de Clèves is aware that, once her husband has died, any obstacle to their love cannot be legitimate in society and in Nemours' eyes:

> *"I know that you are free, that I am free, and that things are of such a kind that the public might have no cause to blame you, nor I either, when we were engaged together for ever. (end of the fourth part)*

The fear of infidelity also stems from the observation that love is fleeting. Indeed, the princess is aware that the Duc de Nemours is a charming man who appeals to many women: "Nothing can prevent me from knowing that you were born with all the dispositions for gallantry and all the qualities that are likely to give happy success there. (end of the fourth part)

In this society, the fidelity and constant love that Mme de Clèves wishes for are not to be found. Thus the maxim that ends the social justification of the Princess of Cleves takes on its full meaning: "One reproaches a lover; but does one reproach a husband, when all one has to do is reproach him for having no love? This maxim, marked by the impersonal and the present tense, highlights the fate of a married woman.

Jealousy, a constituent of passion

All this social argument is reinforced by the inevitable appearance of a destructive feeling, jealousy. The princess fears this emotion, which would prevent her from concealing her passion.

> *"I would be in mortal pain, and I would not even be sure of not having the misfortune of jealousy. I have told you too much to hide from you that you made me aware of it and that I suffered such cruel pain [...] that an idea of it has remained with me which makes me believe that it is the greatest of all evils. (end of the fourth part)*

The hyperboles highlighted show that she will not stand being betrayed. Furthermore, they support the social reasons that make their union impossible. The superlative describes jealousy as an evil superior to any other affliction, against which one can never fight. The hyperbolic expression thus expresses the mismatch between the world of the court and the values of the princess.

"There are few whom you do not please; my experience would lead me to believe that there are none whom you cannot please" (end of the fourth part). By using this litote, the narrator attenuates the statement in order to make it stronger. The Duke of Nemours could not resist a new passion similar to the one he feels for her. As a result, the social argument convinces the reader and the princess of the need to leave the court and legitimises the observation of an impossible love. The young woman thus advocates moral values instilled by her mother which she wishes to preserve.

The duty

Even if she gives in (gives in?) to her passion, apart from the unfortunate consequences of the marital union, her duty and her sense of guilt will (would?) pursue her forever:

> *"When I could get used to this kind of misfortune, could I get used to the misfortune of believing that Monsieur de Cleves would always blame you for his death; reproach me for having loved you, for having married you [...]" (end of the fourth part)*

The use of the hypothetical conditional emphasises that, even if she could overcome jealousy and infidelity, the strength of her duty would not allow her to go against her values and virtue: "It is impossible," she continued, "to get over such strong reasons: I must remain in the state I am in, and in the resolutions I have made never to get out of it." (end of part 4) The social and personal arguments justify Mme de Clèves' final decision to withdraw from the court.

A TRAGIC CHARACTER

All this proves that the heroine can be considered as belonging to the category of tragic characters. First of all, the Cornelian dilemma between passion and duty is characteristic of classical tragedies. These imply that love is impossible. It is true that the princess gradually discovers the passion she feels for the Duke of Nemours and realises that this feeling is insurmountable. She cannot, by her will, thwart her fate: "My destiny did not want me to enjoy this happiness [...]" (end of Part IV) Her passion cannot be controlled even if she has the will. Mme de Clèves is predestined to withdraw from the world in which her values cannot be maintained.

Secondly, the lexical fields give the end of the book a tragic dimension. Unhappiness is essential to the dynamism of the passage and allows the reader to sense the fate of the main character. The term 'misfortune' is frequently used, as well as the terms 'pain' and 'suffering', which contribute to the tragic force. In classical tragedy, love and passion are linked. But passion is also linked to unhappiness, and if Mme de Clèves were to give in to her passions, she would be unhappy.

AVENUES FOR REFLECTION

SOME QUESTIONS FOR FURTHER REFLECTION

- The story is presented as a historical account of the time of Henry II. What advantages does this give the novel?

- Why does the silence of the Princess of Cleves when her portrait is stolen reveal her feelings for the Duke of Nemours?

- What do the house in Coulommiers and the retreat in the Pyrenees have in common?

- If you judge by appearances in this place," replied Mme de Chartres, "you will often be deceived: what appears is almost never the truth. (p. 75). Name some moments in the plot when appearances hide reality.

- How does the anecdote about Mr.^{me} de Tournon inform the main plot?

- What links can be established between the adventure of the vidame described in the lost letter and that of the Princess of Cleves (pp. 129-132)?

- What is the function of reflexive slow motion?

- Why do people say that *The Princess of Cleves* is above all 'a meditation on love'?

- What differences can be observed between the content of *The Princess of Cleves* and the medieval vision of courtly love?

- What similarities could be established between the plot of *The Princess of Cleves* and that of Rousseau's *The New Heloise*?

- How does our story differ from Flaubert's *Madame Bovary* and Stendhal's *The Red and the Black*?

TO GO FURTHER

REFERENCE EDITION

LA FAYETTE Madame de, *The Princess of Cleves*, Paris, Librairie Générale Française, 1999.

BENCHMARK STUDIES

BEAUMARCHAIS J.-P. de and Couty D., *Dictionnaire des grandes œuvres de la littérature française*, Paris, Larousse-VUEF, 2001, pp. 1014-1018.

BENAC H., *Guide des idées littéraires*, Paris, Hachette, 1988.

BIET C., *La tragédie*, Paris, Armand Colin, 1997.

Dantzig C., *Dictionnaire égoïste de la littérature française*, Paris, Grasset, 2005, pp. 823-825.

Duchêne R., « Madame de La Fayette », in POLET J.-C. (ed.), *Patrimoine littéraire européen. Avènement de l'équilibre européen (1616-1720)*, Brussels, De Boeck, 1996, pp. 731-737.

NIEDERST A., La Princesse de Clèves: *le roman paradoxal*, Paris, Librairie Larousse, 1973.

ROUSSET J., *Formes et significations: essais sur les structures littéraires de Corneille à Claudel*, Paris, Librairie José Corti, 1982.

Your opinion is important to us!
Leave a comment on the website of your online bookshop
and share your favourites on social networks!

Although the editor makes every effort to verify the accuracy of the information published, BrightSummaries.com accepts no responsibility for the content of this book.

www.brightsummaries.com

Ebook EAN: 9782808686495
Paperback EAN: 9782808697897
Legal Deposit: D/2023/12603/1069

Cover: © Primento
Digital conception by Primento, the digital partner of publishers.